Chicke
on the Move

by Pam Pollack and Meg Belviso

Illustrated by Lynn Adams

The Kane Press
New York

Book Design/Art Direction: Roberta Pressel

Library of Congress Cataloging-in-Publication Data

Pollack, Pam.
    Chickens on the move / by Pam Pollack and Meg Belviso; illustrated by Lynn Adams.
      p. cm. — (Math matters.)
    Summary: Tom, Anne, and Gordon learn about shape and measurement when they try to find the right spot for their chicken pen.
    ISBN 1-57565-113-0 (pbk. : alk. paper)
    [1. Shape—Fiction. 2. Measurement—Fiction. 3. Chickens—Fiction.] I. Belviso, Meg. II. Adams, Lynn, ill. III. Title. IV. Series.
  PZ7.P7568 Ch 2002
  [E]—dc21
2001038804
                                                 CIP
                                               AC

10 9 8 7 6 5 4 3 2 1

First published in the United States of America in 2002 by The Kane Press.
Printed in Hong Kong.

MATH MATTERS is a registered trademark of The Kane Press.

"Tom! Anne! Gordon!" called Mrs. Dunne.
"Grandpa's here! He has a surprise for you!"
"What is it, Mom?" asked Anne.

"Look!" said her brother Tom. "Chickens!"
"Are they pets?" asked Gordon. "For us?"
The chickens ruffled their feathers and
squawked.

"You bet," Grandpa said. "And we'll have fresh eggs whenever we want."

"Where will they live?" asked Gordon.

"I'm going to build them a house," said Grandpa. "You kids can make a coop. That's like a yard with a fence around it."

"Where should we put the coop?" Anne said.

"How about next to Grandpa's vegetable garden?" said Tom. "Or up on the hill?"

"Let's put it next to the house," said Anne. "That way we'll be able to see the chickens all the time—even when we're inside."

"Could they stay in my room?" Gordon asked.

Anne and Tom smiled.

"Not really," Tom said.

They carried the fence around to the side of the house.

"I'll roll it out," said Anne.

"I'll work on the posts," said Tom.

"I'll talk to the chickens," said Gordon.

9

3

3

9

When they were finished, they had a long, narrow rectangle. It was 9 feet long and 3 feet wide.

"That's the skinniest chicken coop I've ever seen," said Grandpa.

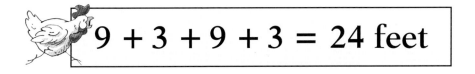

$9 + 3 + 9 + 3 = 24$ feet

Grandpa set the chickens down inside
the coop. They walked back and forth,
clucking and pecking at the grass.

"I still wish they could stay in my room,"
Gordon said.

"Earth to Gordon!" said Tom. "Chickens aren't house pets!"

"They have to stay in a coop," Grandpa said. "An outdoor coop."

"Besides," said Anne, "look how happy they are. They like it out here."

"*Buck, buck, buck,*" said the chickens.

Before he went to bed, Gordon looked out his window.

"Good night, chickens," he called.

Tom and Anne leaned out their windows, too. "Sleep tight, chickens," called Anne.

"Don't let the bedbugs bite," called Tom.
The chickens didn't answer. They were
already asleep.

13

Buck, buck, buck was the first thing Gordon heard the next morning. He raced outside.

Mom and Dad were already there. So were Grandpa, Tom, and Anne. Nobody looked happy.

"I thought chickens were quiet," said Anne.

"Now I'm glad they didn't stay in my room," said Gordon.

"Maybe we should move the chickens next to Grandpa's garden," Tom said.

"Then they wouldn't wake us up," said Anne.

This time they made the chicken coop a little wider. The job took longer than anyone thought it would. The hardest part was catching the chickens!

"Maybe these are racing chickens," said Tom, panting.

8

4

4

8

"I'm *really* glad they aren't staying in my room," thought Gordon. "There would be feathers all over the place."

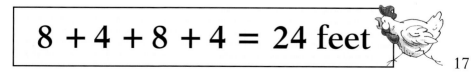

$$8 + 4 + 8 + 4 = 24 \text{ feet}$$

A little later Grandpa decided to water his vegetables. He sprayed the tomatoes, the string beans, and the zucchini. He also sprayed the chickens.

"Whoops!" said Grandpa.

"I guess chickens don't like getting wet," Gordon said.

"We'd better move the coop away from the garden," said Anne.

"Maybe we should put the chickens on the hill," said Tom.

"That's far from the garden," said Anne.

"And the house," said Gordon.

At the top of the hill they made a square coop that was 6 feet on each side.

6

6

6

6

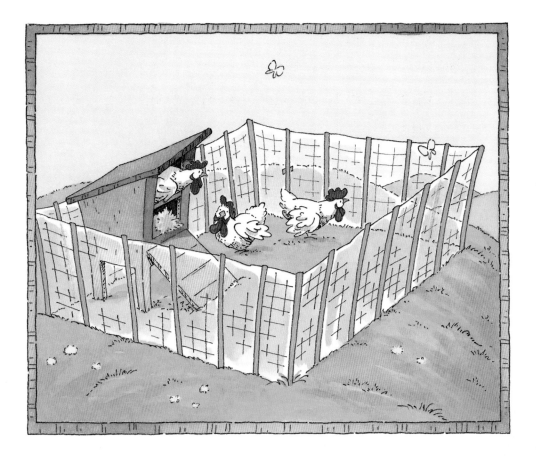

"Now the chickens have more room to play," said Anne.

"They won't get splashed," Gordon said.

"And they won't wake us up," said Tom.

"Maybe they'll like it here," Anne said.

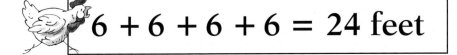

6 + 6 + 6 + 6 = 24 feet

The next morning Grandpa said, "Hey, kids! Check out the coop. There might be a surprise." He was right. There were three eggs.

"One each," said Tom.

"I'll carry them," said Gordon.

"Careful," said Anne.

Gordon tried to be careful, but he tripped and dropped the eggs. They started rolling away.

"Get them!" shouted Tom. But the eggs were rolling too fast. They rolled down the hill and into the pond.

Tom fished the eggs out of the pond. "Good thing they didn't break," he said.

"One's smaller than the others," said Anne.

"It's a funny little egg," Gordon said.

"Let's bring them up to the house," said Tom.

"And let's get something to drink," said Gordon. "I'm thirsty."

"We'd better find another place for the chickens," Anne said. "It's a long trip up and down the hill."

"Especially if I trip!" said Gordon.

"We tried near the house, we tried next to the garden, and we tried up on the hill," said Tom. "What's left?"

They walked all around. Anne stopped between the apple tree and the garage. "Let's try putting it here." she said.

But no matter how they tried, the coop just wouldn't fit.

"Now what?" said Tom.

"Does a coop have to have four sides?" asked Gordon.

Tom and Anne thought hard. "No," they said.

"Then why don't we make it with three sides?" Gordon said.

"Why didn't we think of that?" said Anne.

The chickens explored their new yard.

"They like it!" said Gordon.

"Each one has its own corner," Tom said.

8

8

8

"It's just perfect," said Anne.

"I'm hungry now," Gordon said.

"No wonder," said Tom. "We never had breakfast."

"Let's go," Anne said.

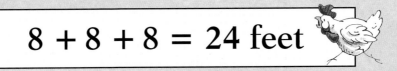

$$8 + 8 + 8 = 24 \text{ feet}$$

"Gordon, do you want the small egg?" asked Mrs. Dunne.

"Okay," Gordon said as he peered at the tiny egg. Suddenly it started to rock back and forth. Then it cracked.

A tiny turtle poked his head out.

"Mom!" Gordon cried. "Can I keep him?"

"Where?" asked Mrs. Dunne.

"In my room," said Gordon.
He had it all figured out.

PERIMETER CHART

The distance around a figure is called its **perimeter**.

You can add the lengths of the sides of a figure to find its perimeter.

Gordon says the perimeter of each figure is 24 feet. Is he right? How do you know?

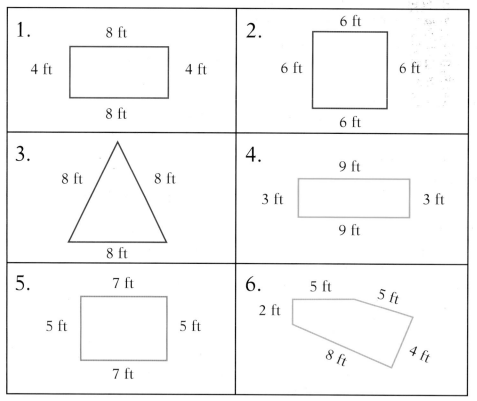

1.
8 ft
4 ft   4 ft
8 ft

2.
6 ft
6 ft   6 ft
6 ft

3.
8 ft   8 ft
8 ft

4.
9 ft
3 ft   3 ft
9 ft

5.
7 ft
5 ft   5 ft
7 ft

6.
5 ft
2 ft   5 ft
8 ft   4 ft